A KITTEN for ROSIE

Written by Erica Frost
Illustrated by Gioia Fiammenghi

Troll Associates

Library of Congress Cataloging in Publication Data

Frost, Erica.
    A kitten for Rosie.

    Summary: Rosie determines to keep her new kitten
despite the landlady's rule against having pets in
the house.
    [1. Cats—Fiction. 2. Pets—Fiction] I. Fiammenghi,
Gioia, ill. II. Title.
PZ7.F92037Ki   1986   [E]   85-14126
ISBN 0-8167-0650-6 (lib. bdg.)
ISBN 0-8167-0651-4 (pbk.)

A KITTEN for ROSIE

"Rosie! Not from your glass!
You'll get germs!"
Rosie's mother put a saucer of
milk on the floor.

"Fluffy's just a baby," said
Rosie. "She's not big enough to
have germs."

The kitten licked the milk with its small, pink tongue.
"Boy," said Rosie, "is she smart! I loved her the second I found her. Isn't she beautiful?"

The kitten licked its paw and
washed its face.
"Did you see that?" said Rosie.
"This kitten is amazing. This
kitten is one hundred percent
clean!"

Rosie's mother laughed.

"Then it's settled," said Rosie.
"She can stay in my room. She'll
be good and quiet. You won't
even know she's here."

HOW
TO
MAKE
JAM

Rosie's mother shook her head.
"I'm sorry, Rosie. You know we
can't keep her. Mrs. Grimby
says *no cats allowed*."

"Who has a cat?" asked Rosie. "Fluffy's a kitten. Do you see a cat?"

"Mrs. Grimby is our landlady,"
said her mother. "She makes the
rules. No kittens or cats—Fluffy
must go."

Rosie made five phone calls.
Jane and Charlene had dogs.
Harry's mother was allergic.
Marjorie's father hated cats.
And Stanley had six cats
already.

Rosie's mother said, "We'll have
to call the animal shelter."

"No!" said Rosie. "I'll take her to the park. I'll find her a good home. I promise."

On the way to the park, Rosie
changed her mind.
"Poor Fluffy," she said. "I won't
give you away. I'll hide you in
Mrs. Grimby's tool shed. No one
will ever find out."

The tool shed needed a cleaning. It smelled of grass clippings and paint. Shovels and rakes and a broken hoe leaned against the walls.

There was a wheelbarrow in one
corner, filled with flowerpots.
There were oily rags and
newspapers and a pair of
Mrs. Grimby's galoshes.

It was not like Mrs. Grimby to
leave all that junk lying around.
Just then, Rosie heard voices.

It was Mrs. Grimby and Calvin,
the boy who mowed the lawn.

Quickly, Rosie dropped Fluffy
into one of the galoshes.

She slipped through the door
and hid behind the shed—just in
time.

"Do a good job," she heard Mrs. Grimby say. "And Calvin, don't forget. Get rid of that trash." While Calvin was busy with the mower, Rosie ran past him and hurried upstairs.

Her mother asked, "Did you
find a good home for Fluffy?"
And Rosie took a deep breath
and answered, "Yes, I did."

When her father came home, he said, "What's the matter with Rosie?"
"I don't know," said her mother. "She's been acting funny all day."

Rosie only picked at her supper.
She was worried. What if her
parents knew she had lied?
What if Mrs. Grimby found out
about Fluffy? And, worst of all,
what if Calvin threw Fluffy out
with the trash?

Rosie went to bed early. But she didn't fall asleep for a long, long time.

In the morning, her eyes were
red.
"Put this on," said her mother.
"It will cheer you up."
She held up Rosie's favorite
dress. The dress was red and
white. When Rosie put it on,
she felt like a candy cane.

Rosie drank her juice. She hid
some of her breakfast in her
napkin. Fluffy would be
hungry. When she thought of
Fluffy, her stomach flopped.

She kissed her mother and ran
down the steps.
"Watch out for your dress," her
mother called after her.

Rosie ran to the tool shed. The door was locked. She twisted the knob. She jiggled it. She shook it. The door would not budge. "What am I going to do?" she said.

There was a window, but it was
too high. Rosie found a box and
stood on it. Then she pushed
with both hands. Slowly, the
window opened.

Rosie was halfway through the
window when she heard
someone humming.

It was Mrs. Grimby. She was
coming to see if Calvin had
cleaned the shed.

Rosie tried to get away, but the
front of her dress caught on a
nail. She pulled this way and
that. Then, all at once, she
tumbled to the ground. Her
dress was ruined.
"Rats!" she said. "What will I
tell my mother?"

When she looked up, Mrs. Grimby was standing over her. "What in the world!" said Mrs. Grimby. She took a key from her pocket and opened the door to the shed.

In the dark shed, something was
moving. Mrs. Grimby looked
closer. One of her galoshes was
rocking back and forth.

"Eeeeeeek!" she shrieked.
"Heaven help us all! I've seen a
ghost!"

From deep within the boot,
came a low, sad moan. Then
the boot fell over. Mrs. Grimby
stared into the face of a very
frightened kitten.

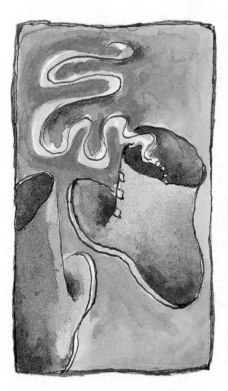

She looked at Rosie.
"Young lady," she said, "what
do you know about this?"

Then Rosie's mother was there.
She looked at Rosie in her torn
dress. She looked at Fluffy.
"Rosie, Rosie, Rosie," she said.
"What am I going to do with
you?"

Rosie began to cry.
"I'm sorry," she said. "I really
am. I only wanted Fluffy to be
safe."

"*Mew*," said Fluffy.
Anyone could see she was
hungry.

"Why doesn't somebody feed
her?" said Mrs. Grimby.
She bent down and patted the
kitten's head.
Rosie held her breath.

"The truth is," said Mrs. Grimby, "I'm sure I saw a mouse in the cellar. Do you think Fluffy could catch a mouse?"

"Oh, yes," said Rosie. "She'll be a fine mouser when she grows up."

"Well, what are we waiting for?" said Mrs. Grimby. "Let's feed her. I can't stand mice!"